UNEARTHLY LONDON

A Fallowgrave Tale

By

TE Hodden

AF486029

Prologue

We met Dee and Grace for the first time on a blustery, drizzly, September afternoon, at a coffee shop in central London,

We were a few minutes late, but the girls were waiting on us, holding a table, and eeking out their coffee and muffins.

Dee was a geography teacher, and a friend of a friend, a warm, bubbly, squirrel of a woman, with an open face and big-sister smile. As writers we moved in some of the same circles, contributing to the same magazine for the last few years, and occasionally to a mutual friend's podcast.

Her girlfriend Grace was the assistant manager for a bookshop, a large branch of a national chain. She was a transwoman, a few years younger than Dee, a demure kingfisher of a woman, with autumnal hair and eyes full of thoughts, dressed in all the colours of the ocean.

Our mutual friend, the features editor of the magazine had arranged the meeting, promising it would be a fun adventure for me.

It was Grace who made the pitch. "We were talking with some of the others about building some podcasts using the magazine's brand, adapting some of the regular columns into short series, and… we wanted to start with Unearthly London."

"Oh," I said. "So… you want to read my columns on a podcast?"

Dee nodded. "We would want to do a little more than that, maybe build on the articles and go into a little more depth, chase down some interviews, or… maybe go looking for the Uncannies ourselves?"

Scamp perked up at that. "Go… looking for them?"

Grace nodded. "Yeah."

Scamp grinned. "Like… the ghosts? And magicians? And… UFOs?"

Grace sighed. "Well, we probably won't find them, but… It would be interesting to try."

Dee looked between us. "So… did you want to?"

Scamp jabbed me with her elbow.

"Sure," I agreed. "Okay."

*

In recent decades there has been something of a resurgence of folklore and mythology in and around London. Long forgotten tall tales, conspiracy theories and urban legends have found a new lease of life on the internet, waking from dormancy to reinvent themselves.

At the same time whole new tall tales and ghost stories have flourished, spreading far, growing deep roots, lodging themselves firmly in the public narrative, resisting any facts or evidence that might debunk or disprove them.

In my column for magazine I called these stories the Unearthly.

This book follows our investigations into the Unearthly tales, in and around London, and our attempts to witness the supernatural, the unexplained, and the mysterious for ourselves. To make a podcast that was never finished.

Part One: The Cities Within The City

The City of London is the ancient heart of London, the old city from which the metropolis has grown, swallowing up towns and villages as it spread outwards.

The City is both woven into the very fabric of London, but also distinct, in that it has its own Mayor, police force, and local governance. It is considered its own county. It houses many historic landmarks, and houses London's Financial Services Industry, in the Central Business District.

Across the river is London's other city within the city, Westminster, the seat of political power, with the Houses of Parliament, Downing Street, and Portcullis House. Westminster is both a borough of London, and a city of its own.

Both these twins were shaped by Victorian engineering, by the building of the Embankments, the engineering of the Thames itself, and by the bridges that bound them together.

Both these cities within the city are saturated in history, in their very fabric, with hints of the past, the Roman and the medieval, woven into the architecture and landscape. Buildings from all periods rub shoulders, and jostle for room with ultra-modern skyscrapers.

These make the cities rich and fertile ground, for myths, legends, and folklore to take shape.

Sir Gimble Grey

It is a bitterly cold November night, and the four of us are sat on a bench, on the embankment, watching the traffic that rumbles across a grand old bridge.

We are on our first vigil, seeking our first brush with the Unearthly.

Scamp is snuggled close, her mop of dyed silver curls resting on my shoulder, her hands tangled in mine, her new camera resting on her lap.

Dee is cuddled up to Grace, as they watch the infra-sound detector on Dee's phone.

Summer stretched all the way through and kissed October, before we suddenly toppled into a deep, frosty, Autumn. There is a cloudless sky tonight, and the frost has painted the city silver, glowing brightly under the light of the full moon.

Saturday night has ticked into Sunday morning, and it is now late enough that the clubs and pubs have closed, and the last of the diehards are making their way to the taxi ranks and hotels, on their shambling, jeering, way home.

A gaggle of girls in hen night fancy dress are on a wayward, staggering course for the bridge, giggling and stumbling on their way.

"Here we go!" Dee says, peeling herself from Scamp, and watching the levels jump on her infra-sound meter.

We all sit forward.

I help Scamp hold the bulky camera steady, as she zooms in on the bridge.

The levels on the infrasound scanner flutter.

The hen party reaches the midpoint of the bridge.

Nothing happens.

They pass to the far side of the river, and head for one of the grand art-deco hotels that loom over the river.

Scamp gives me a disappointed look, and slumps against me. "Are we sure its tonight?"

"Yeah," I answer. "Pretty sure."

Scamp gives me a playful scowl. "Well that doesn't inspire confidence."

"Hey!" I hold up a defensive hand. "It's tonight. I did the maths."

"Oh?" Scamp narrows her eyes. "Like you did with the wallpaper for the hall?"

I sigh and settle against her.

Grace is trying not to laugh, *really* trying.

Dee shows us the phone. "Well, if tonight isn't the night, there is something really weird going on with these readings."

*

Stories of Sir Gimble Grey first went viral in 2009, appearing in some of the spooky corners of social media, that were picked up content hungry news feeds.

According to the legend Sir Gimble Grey was a stuffy and starched civil servant, working late on New Years Eve, 1962. Sometime after midnight he tried to make his way home, but as he made his way through the revelling crowd somebody bumped into him, and gave him a drunken shove, into the path of a passing taxi.

At some point after (the story is a little vague on exactly when) Gimble Grey started appearing on the bridge, on nights with a full moon, lurching out of groups of pedestrians, and into the paths of cars.

The version that spread quickly through the internet gave three different accounts of people who had allegedly seen the ghost.

But that isn't where this story gets strange.

Almost as soon as the story began to circulate, fact checking sites found that there was a good reason why no trace of Grey, his death, or any of the people in the three incidents. They were from a radio play, broadcast in the late nineties, as part of an anthology series.

Which would be a good reason to take any subsequent story of encountering the ghost with a ladle sized pinch of salt.

And yet… there really were reports made to the police, of drivers, screeching to a halt as a hefty, balding, gent in pinstripes who crashed through a bunch of pedestrians, and fell in front of their car. The calls were from distraught drivers, and panicked pedestrians, terrified that they couldn't find somebody they were sure was hit.

There was every possibility of an elaborate hoax, of course, but the Police Officers seemed to have believed the witnesses.

And incidents still happen, more or less as the stories describe.

This is how my Aunt Teddy covered one such incident, in an article accompanied by an eerie screen shot from a traffic camera, that showed a car slamming to a halt on the bridge, and shocked looking pedestrians reacting to a misty blur in the middle of the road:

Ghost Caught On Film?

The ghost stories of Sir Gimble Grey have long been debunked as the plot from D.D. Schreiber's play 'A Slave To Circumstance', apparently nobody told the ghost. Despite never having lived, the ill fated Civil Servant continues to haunt Westminster Bridge, and may have been caught on film.

Mr D Rhys, a taxi driver, had a close encounter. He says: "I was crossing the bridge on my way to collect a client, when a small group walking the other way flail in a commotion, and somebody leapt from their group into the road. I distinctly glimpsed a heavy set man in a suit and bowler hat, and I felt the impact as I slammed on the brakes, but when I got out the car to help, he had just vanished. I thought he had gone into the river, so we called the police, expecting there to be a search."

A police helicopter with a thermal camera was summoned, and a police boat was soon searching the area, but when the responding officer had the footage from the traffic cameras reviewed, there was no portly gentleman to be seen, just a strange ethereal blur.

Ms R. Lovelace, a witness to the event, says: "It was definitely a man. Five of us were walking across the bridge, which had been empty, when I suddenly felt this shove, as something came from the shadows, and barged through our group. He was a bulbous older man, with grey hair, in a suit and hat. He stumbled into the road and went under the car, but then he was just...gone."

A spokesman for the Metropolitan Police says that a full search for the victim on and around the bridge was carried out, but unsuccessful. The investigation is ongoing.

Over the years, reports of accidents, or near misses with Gimble Grey on the bridge, under a full moon, have continued at a steady enough pace that attending one of the searches has become a rite of passage for probationary police officers.

So, this raised the question: If hauntings were being witnessed, could they have predated the radio play? Perhaps the author, D.D, Schreiber had been inspired by some pre-existing phenomena?

"No," he told me, in no uncertain terms, a week before the vigil. He was on the other end of a midmorning video-call, sat at the kitchen table in his Edinburgh townhouse. "I am afraid I made it all up. Originally I had written something completely different, but the script editor was worried it was too similar to another episode of the series, so I volunteered to rewrite it. I thought of the scariest thing that happened in my life, which was when a dog bolted from the hedgerow and in front of my car. I slammed on the brakes, but it was too close for me to do anything, and it was maybe a million to one chance that it had got to the other side of the road unharmed, but those few seconds, with my heart running a thousand miles an hour, not knowing if I had hit the poor beast or not, was… absolutely terrifying. Anyway, I was living in London at the time, so I set the play there, and I tapped into the idea of somebody bolting in front of a car, and… London Bridge sounded too cliched, so I shifted it to Westminster, and… that was it."

"So, do you see it as an endorsement of your writing that people think it was real?"

"I think it shows I did something right. Although… I wouldn't mind the kind of success that makes you money." He laughed. "Actually, I have a theory about what might be going on."

"Oh?" I asked.

"So…" Schreiber gestured with his hands. "Jillderay Magic. The power of perception and personal reality. Somebody took my play and posted it around, pretending it was real, and maybe just enough people believed it, that when something happened they were primed to think it was Gimble. And *those* stories go around, and more people believe it, and maybe when enough people believe it, the idea reaches critical mass, and sooner or later you have people *making* Gimble real, or… at least real for them."

The idea of a fiction resonating so much that people experienced elements of it, as though they were real, is not without precedent.

Elsewhere in London is a set of steps, the last remaining part of a previous London Bridge, said to be haunted by an entirely fictional murder from the pen of Charles Dickens, and a railway cutting said to be haunted by the spectre of an 'accident' staged for a public information film (that, to be fair, did terrify an entire generation of school kids away from trespassing on railway lines, and was pretty darned nightmare inducing).

In Kent, there is a stately home said to be haunted by the apparition of a reanimated Egyptian Mummy, the historically inaccurate monster of a nearly forgotten slice of nineteen sixties B Movie horror.

Incidents such as these suggest, that some hauntings are purely the result of human psychology, born from the same evolutionary instincts that let us see faces in clouds, or convince ourselves of the monster under the bed. Our prehistoric ancestors who caught a movement, or a shadow, in the corner of their eye, and interpreted it as a threat lived longer than those who ignored it. These once life saving instincts still linger, hard wired into our brains, and perhaps, if we see a movement that might be somebody about to step into the path of a car, especially when we have been primed with stories that there is a guy who does just that, our brains will interpret the blur as a figure, and we will react accordingly.

Of course, how we could begin to test and challenge this theory is beyond me.

*

As dawn approaches we bring our vigil to an end, and rise to our feet. We stretch out and walk in the vague direction of the car park.

"So…" Scamp says, with a yawn. "Should I be relieved, or saddened, that we didn't see him?"

"A little of both?" Grace suggests.

We laugh.

Dee perks up. "I know somewhere we can go for coffee."

"Oooh!" Scamp huddles in her coat. "A hot chocolate would be nice."

The tea wagon is in the entrance to a walled garden, one of the small parks and green spaces scattered through the city. There is a small crowd of taxi drivers are there, sipping cups of tea or coffee, and warming their fingers.

While I buy a round of drinks, Grace talks to the drivers. All of them know somebody who claims to have seen Gimble, but none have seen him themselves.

We take our drinks and amble back to the street.

A shrill tone rings out, filling the early morning. It takes me a reason to realise that it is coming from the red phone box on the corner.

I look around at the apartment buildings that overlooked the phone box. "Somebody has the wrong number." And then I realise. "And if they keep ringing back, it's just going to disturb everybody."

Scamp gives me one of her looks.

I step over and pick up the phone. "Hello?"

The other end of the line is silent.

"Hello," I repeat. "I think you have the wrong number. This is a public phone."

There is a scratching noise over the line, the hiss and pop of an old record being played, and a jaunty little tune, a sea shanty played in strings and brass.

I hang up.

Scamp raises a bemused eyebrow as I step out the box. "What was that?"

I shake my head. "Some kind of prank call, with music?"

She shrugs. "Weird."

The phone does not ring again.

The four of us walk back to the car.

Curtvile Moorealan

The autumn of 1888 was a scary time to be a Londoner.

In the East End there was a plague of twelve murders that the Press connected as the Whitechapel Murders. Detectives quickly deduced that five of those murders were committed by one hand, the unknown killer known in the Press as Jack the Ripper.

Elsewhere another killer was at large. Between 1887 and 1889 bits and pieces of four victims, only one of whom was eventually identified, were found in or around the Thames (including one found in the building site of New Scotland Yard). This series of murders, is variously known as the Thames Mysteries, or the Thames Torso Murders.

These too, were unsolved.

Even scarier is that there were other murders, from as early as 1873, to as late as 1902, that are similar enough for some to speculate if they were connected.

In the middle of this Autumn of Terror, a mob descended on cemetery, broke open a family vault, and dragged out the coffin and mouldering bones of a man who died nearly three decades earlier, on Christmas Eve 1860, setting upon the body and casket with sledgehammers, tossing the remains onto a raging bonfire.

Witnesses, writing at the time, described flocks of crows circling overhead, singing a lament as the smoke from the bonfire turned as black as tar.

The body being burned was that of Curtvile Moorealan.

A rumour had spread through London, no more than a whisper, that Moorealan had been seen stalking the backstreets and alleyways, and that was enough to spur the mob to action, to be sure that he couldn't be back.

Even in death, Moorealan had a powerful grip on London, and the world.

This was not the end of his story, however, nor the last time he would be seen.

*

Moorealan was born in Hull, at sunset on Twelfth Night, in 1800. His family were poor labourers, and in his own words (taken from his diaries), he knew the 'misery and cruelty of poverty, and the miserable cruelty of those who maintain it, to secure their own power'.

Although he had little formal education, Moorealan was literate, and absorbed information like a sponge. Any conversation he heard, or overheard, any snippet he read, or story he was told, got absorbed and stored. More than this, he was a talented artist and writer.

Joining a theatre troupe as a young man, apprenticed to the set builder, but he was afforded the chance to write, adding his dramas to their insatiable need for fresh drama. By the time he turned forty, he was writing not only for his own comrades, but under a dozen pseudonyms, he wrote plays and skits for other troupes, and scores of serials, for the flourishing press.

It was a stage illusionist however, master of sleight of hand and grand magic, that he became best known.

It was within Moorealan's lifetime that the art of stage illusion was revolutionised, and Robert-Houdin created the archetypical magician as a gentleman in formal dress. Moorealan dressed in the then traditional trappings of a sorcerer or wizard to perform his magic, although his dress was informed by images of the prehistoric tribes of Britain, with a cape of furs, and shamanic airs. His patter was informed by the beliefs of the Jillderay school of magic, using ritual and ceremony to alter personal perceptions, and thus the nature of reality.

Some would argue that his on stage patter was unique, and better informed by the countless others claiming to have learned ancient secrets from wise men in far off lands. He wrapped his acts in history and legends, both familiar to his audience, but also strangely alien. He spoke convincingly of having looked into the past, of having seen Boudicca riding to battle, or Alfred on the run.

Others would say that he mixed all too real rituals and true magic into his rituals.

Imagine him now, emerging from the smoke and shadows on the gloomy stage, a rangy, powerfully built man, with a strong accent, and rich voice, long hair and full beard, his eyes bright and vital, surrounded by shadows, dressed in quilted armour, studded with steel, beneath his long cloak of fur and leather, his talon fingers armoured in countless rings.

His illusions were stunning, more so because he never shared the mechanics with a soul. Nobody inherited his methods, or built upon his legacy, as far as anybody can tell, his illusions were all unique.

In one, he would have shadow puppets projected onto the screen. He would pluck the shadows from the screen, and carry them across the stage, casting them away into the flames of a fire.

In another he would take a stub of a candle, and rejuvenate it into fresh and virgin wax, as a bowl of fruit spoiled and rotted to nothing in a matter of seconds.

Moorealan's talents earned him not only considerable acclaim, but wealth and status. He purchased a fine townhouse, with ample space for his work, and moved through the highest circles of society, where he acquired a reputation for his Unearthly knowledge and insight. It was said that if he stared into somebody's eyes, none of their secrets were safe.

A Lord, who met him at a social engagement, described the experience thus:

He was pointed out to me from across the room, a looming fellow, rangy, beaky, and wild haired. He was dressed as precisely as a dandy, but all in black, his shirt, his waistcoat, and jacket, even his tie, his fingers festooned in silver. He was talking to some fellow or other about politics, or history, or the price of lumber in the Americas. Anybody could ask anything of him, and he would know enough to impress.

Then a lady I shall call S caught his eye.

S took him to the gardens, and thinking I had the scent of useful scandal I quite accidentally happened to find myself taking air in a side passage, out of sight but within earshot of them.

"The man I love," said S, "is at sea. I will not see him for many months, and I worry."

Moorealan chuckled. "And I am sure the good Lieutenant worries for your safety too."

There was a telling silence.

The S enquired. "Is it possible to know if he is safe?"

"Do you have any coins?" Enquired Moorealan. "One of silver and one of copper?"

By chance, S did.

I risked a peek out around the corner, satisfied neither could see me.

S dropped her coins into the magician's wineglass, and through some stage trickery, perhaps a chemical reaction from some agent slipped into the wine by sleight of hand, the wine bubbled and boiled, belching acrid steam into the air.

Moorealan placed his hand over the glass, stilling the reaction. He tilted his head back, and stared up to the stars. "I see that the lieutenant will be home safe, after you have started to show your condition, but long before his daughter is born. She will be fair haired, with your mother's eyes, and his father's wisdom."

S seemed satisfied, and scampered away.

Moorealan poured away his wine. The coins seemed to have vanished. Without turning, he raised his voice so that I could hear. "A stolen secret is a terrible thing, My Lord, and best forgotten, or kept silent."

"You dare threaten me?" I demanded, with a scoff.

He turned to look at me, and I swear his gaze turned the air cold. "No, My Lord. I warn you. An ill gotten secret is dangerous. If you are careless, or worse, if you try to use it to your advantage, then Truth will hurt you back, and you... My Lord, have so many truths that should remain... confidential."

I almost laughed. "Oh, do I?"

He stared into my eyes.

I do not know why I stepped back, or why I felt so suddenly cold. I do not know why my heart stopped and my breath burned in my craw. Why my knees buckled, or why I could not look away from his eyes.

"I am not your enemy, My Lord," he said, softly and gently, "but I do ask your word that what you heard here will remain in confidence."

"Of course," I stammered.

And with those words, I could breathe once more, and my heart hammered against my ribs.

Moorealan's three most recognised, and enduring, novels were all written and published in the year before his death. 'The Werewolf Of The Weald', 'The Widow's Dawn', and 'A Man Of Many Riddles', all had modest success in their day, but would have a far longer, far more enduring appeal for decades after. His stage persona long retired, and no longer writing dramas, he invested all his creative efforts into his novels.

On Christmas Eve of 1860, Moorealan was invited to address a small, but notable, audience in Westminster. He spoke at length about his childhood, his apprenticeship in the theatre industry, and the creation of his magical persona. He revealed nothing of his tricks, or illusion, but he spoke with a passion of the historical, occult, and mythological influences on that aspect of his self.

Having finished his talk, he made his way around the room, finding time to talk to everybody, answer their questions, and thank them for their rapt attention.

Then, as he went outside to find his cabs a stranger pushed their way through the crowd, and shot him twice in the back. The suspect fled, and vanished, never to be discovered.

It was twenty years later, that Moorealan's life and reputation underwent some strange transformations, when his personal journals were found.

Personally, having seen the originals on display at a museum, I happen to be convinced that they were written by Moorealan, but I do not believe they were ever meant to be an accurate record of his life, nor indeed, that they were anything other than one of his most wonderful flights of fantasy and imagination.

Others disagree.

The journals largely describe Moorealan's life, in considerable detail, but without warning, but woven seamlessly into these events are magical encounters with ghosts, fairies, and other beings. Moorealan makes the acquaintance of a mysterious, raggedy, gentleman, with a youthful body, but eyes that have seen many centuries. The gentleman is Mister Retsim, a master of the Jillderay school of magic, who takes Moorealan under his wing, teaching him all kinds of magic, that lead to many exciting adventures: communing with angels, communing with trolls, casting away dark spirits, and the ritual of transformation, required to become a werewolf.

To modern eyes it is a simple story, written as Moorealans personal passion, a great novel intended for no audience but himself, for his own amusement.

Some saw it as a confession of dark and terrible powers.

Wild and weird rumours began to circulate. One diarist at the time recorded with glee how she had heard tell from her servants that Moorealan had often been found scouring the city for stray cats and dogs, whose blood and flesh would be used in terrible rituals, and that he had hypnotised many men into making false confessions, knowing that once they went to the gallows, his secrets would be safe.

By the Autumn of Terror, some people only knew his name in association with the tales of dark magic, curses, and werewolves.

There may have been a seed of truth to one of these rumours.

Moorealan was indeed known to search the streets for stray cats, although with far more charitable intentions. He kept the company of many cats in his house, over the years, treating them well, and often nursing them from the edge of death to ruddy health.

In the nineteen thirties, Moorealan would undergo another transformation…

*

I meet Willow Svenson for lunch in a small Italian restaurant, tucked away on the back streets. Willow is in her early thirties, prim, and professional, in a dark trouser suit, and horn rimmed glasses.

She takes a deep breath, before she starts talking. "So… I was seventeen, fresh out of school, and in my first real job, as a waitress for a catering company, and this function I had been working at had finished late. I was dead on my feet, aching all over, and just wanted to get home to sleep. It had been one of those nights where some of the guests had been that special kind of arsehole, who has to treat the little people like crap, just to assure their mates how superior and above it all they are. You know?"

I nod. "I think I've met a few of them."

She shrugs. "So, I flop onto the train, and plug in my headphones, and sink down into my own little world. I don't even register, at first, that there's a cat sitting opposite me. It's hardly the weirdest thing I've ever seen on the Underground. Anyway, this bunch of guys from the function stagger onto the platform, so drunk they are sweaty and seasick. They crash onto the train, into my carriage as the doors are beeping, so I don't have time to move, or get out. Their stink, and their too-loud squawking laughter fills the whole carriage. And then…" She looks away, her expression growing heavy. "And then the train moves, and one of them stumbles over, and loses his balance. He thumps against me, and as he stands up, he's raging, screaming at me to mind out, and not be so clumsy. He looks at his shoes, and turns purple, furious. He starts going on about how I scuffed them, and how much they cost, and…"

"Are you okay?" I ask.

She nods. "I try to walk down the carriage, but he follows me, demanding to know what I'm going to do to pay for his shoes. His mates are all balling with laughter. They think its hilarious. As the train pulls into Westminster, I've decided I'm getting off. I'll wait for another train, or get a taxi, or… something. So… I hop off, as soon as the train stops. But he follows me, still raging and screaming at me, because I owe him… some stupid amount of money. And suddenly I realise I'm alone of the platform, and the train is pulling away." She shudders. "I see the emergency and information point and run for it, but he catches my wrist, and… for a moment I am terrified that this is how I die, but… he stops, and… we aren't alone on the platform anymore. First I see the cat from the train. Then I see he isn't alone. There are dozens of cats, all hunched up and hissing at the guy, with sharp teeth and claws. But the guy? He isn't looking at the cats. He's looking at the man stood down the platform, staring at us. He's tall, and lanky, but powerful, with a beard and long hair, wearing a leather and fur cape over a smart, but old fashioned suit. The stranger holds up a hand, and points at the thug, and… the thug lets go of my wrist, and backs away, right the way back until he is teetering on the edge of the platform. The older guy makes another gesture and the thug stands there, straining and shaking, like he is struggling against something, but can't move. The cats all march forwards, surrounding the thug, and… I just run." She laughs and rubs her face. "And it's only when I reach the surface, that I dare think it could have been Moorealan. But who else could it be? I know he is meant to protect the homeless, but maybe he took pity on me too, and… who else could he be? With the beard, and the cats, and… the magic?"

I don't know how to answer that. "You had heard the stories?"

"Everybody heard the stories when I grew up." Willow softens her voice. "There was an old guy, homeless, camping in the railway cutting behind the school. Some of the kids used to throw bottles and cans down at his stuff, trying to drive him off. Adults didn't just tell them off, they warned them that he would be under Moorealan's protection. He always protects the strays. Moorealan was like… a bogeyman to enforce the rules. I don't think I ever believed it, but…I knew the stories. That those who wronged him had once chance to back away and learn to be better, as the next time you saw him, there would be no warning."

Stories of people having seen Moorealan began in the thirties, and continued, sporadically, since. He was sometimes seen in and around Westminster and the Embankment, stalking the streets where he had often walked, deep in thought, seeking inspiration, or at the site of his murder, but more often he was seen throughout London, by those in need of a guardian angel.

Most often he was glimpsed only as a tall, thin, watching over a pride of well looked after cats. Other times he was a protective presence, warning off those who intend harm to a lonely traveller, or one of London's homeless.

At other times he was an interested passer by, who would stop to talk to artists, photographers, or those taking the time to look carefully at London's architecture.

"Have you seen him again?" I ask.

Willow chuckles. "The ghost or the cat?" She looks away. "I've seen the cat since, riding the trains. Quite a few times. Often enough for me to start carrying a little bag of treats in my handbag. He's nice, but I don't think he wants me to adopt him, although I have offered, a couple of times."

The Westminster Shadow

"Is it Dee?" Asks Ernie McShane, as he wanders over.

Dee and I have just stepped into The Yeoman, McShane's local, in the shadow of a railway embankment, a short walk from Lewisham High Street. We are a few minutes early for our meeting, but Ernie is already settled at a table in the corner, nearing the bottom of a pint of mild.

Dee nods and makes the introduction.

"Another of those?" I ask.

Ernie nods, and downs the remnants. "Lovely, thanks. Shall we?"

Ernie looks like a sergeant of the Templar Knights, born to the wrong century, broad and stocky, with a shaven scalp and iron wool beard, broken by a friendly smile, a few tattoos peeking out from the sleeves of his sweater.

By the time I get a round in, Dee has her recorder out, and is ready to go with the interview.

Ernie perches a pair of horn rimmed glasses on his nose. "So… you want to know about *it* don't you?"

Dee smiles. "If… you are happy to tell us."

Ernie shrugs. "Well… I can tell you what I saw, and what people said at the time, but I don't much about the old stories. We never knew about the Shadow, or… any of that. I still don't know if that is what we saw. On the job, we used to call it Hobb. I reckon it was old Johnny and Townsend who came up with that. They loved old movies, you know? I think the name came from one of their crappy old horror movies."

I glance at Dee.

"So," she says, "you were working on the extension to the underground railway, ahead of the millennium?"

Ernie nods. "1997 or 98. It was good work. The problems began on the Westminster stretch. The first thing you should know is that… yes… there are a lot of stories about the tunnels being haunted, but in my experience it was always a bit of joke. Work down there for any length of time, and you get a feel for why its spooky. A train rumbling past in one tunnel can cause air movements, or rumbling in another, unconnected tunnel, that can make odd sounds, or a door swing itself open, then closed, the railway itself plays tricks. So the thing is… when genuinely weird stuff happens we notice, and people try and laugh it off, but… little mistakes can make big trouble. Little accidents can get somebody hurt. Or killed. So… yeah… when little things start happening, people notice."

I ask: "What sort of little things?"

"Things that should be locked being found open,"
Ernie said. "Or lights being switched off while
somebody is trying to work. Or…lots of little things,
that just didn't add up. At first we thought it was some
contractor trying to cover mistakes, but then I took
responsibility for stuff, and it still happened, when it
just… *couldn't*. Padlocks opened themselves, under our
noses, and equipment turned itself off, behind locked
doors. Then we started finding… electrical supply
boxes crusted in ice, when they should be running hot,
and tools bent out of shape. So… when people started
talking about the gargoyle shadow, I believed them."

Dee nods. "Then you saw it?"

Ernie hesitates. He sips his drink. "Then I saw it." He lowers his voice. "There was an issue with one of the power lines. I went to the substation, to reset the breakers. It isn't dark, or dingy, or claustrophobic. Its big, and airy, and full of light, bright, clean, and brand new. But I have the weirdest feeling of being watched. So, I reset the breaker, and when I turn around, to fill out the logbook, there is a shadow on the wall, that doesn't belong to me, or anybody. The others called it a gargoyle, and… it didn't look like one, but it looked more like one of those than a man. It was long, and thin, with talon finger, and a head like an eagle, something on the shoulders that might be wings or a cloak…" He sips his drink, and chuckles. "Well, I scream, and stagger away, and lock the door, and… just run up to the surface for air, and… I didn't go back, because… I know it sounds stupid, it being a shadow, and I know everybody has some theory about what I *really* saw, but it was staring at me, it was watching me… I never went back. I quit and took any job I could, as long as it weren't there…" He shook his head. "And these days, on the internet, you read stories about people seeing it up above ground, and... I always wonder who, or what, it is looking for. Mostly, I want to not be there when it finds it."

Dee looks at him. "Some of the stories talk about the gift of vision, or nightmares, did you¬"

"No!" Ernie snaps the word far too quickly. He tries to compensate with a laugh, but it is a hollow and unconvincing sound. "No, those are just... stories."

*

'The Faversham Lament' is nearly forgotten now, but in the 1660s it was a popular play. It may not have been a classic to rival Shakespeare, or Marlowe's work, indeed, we don't even know who wrote it, but in its time it was a popular work, adopted by many travelling troupes, perfect for playing in modest sized venues.

In one passage, a sailor describes having seen the ravages of plague upon London:

Empty streets are owned, by the carrion crow and hungry rat, haunted by the weary and broken, buckling under the weight of their defeat. Every window is barred, by shutters nailed closed, every door locked, marked by the devil's own red claw, with a mockery of the cross.

And yes, the tales of the winged shadow, watching from the darkness, are too often told. Drawn as it is, from the depths of the clay beneath our feet, by the stench of death that lingers on the air.

This is our earliest reference to the Westminster Shadow, but it assumes the audience will recognise the reference, which suggests the legend was already well established, and written into lore. It seems likely that myth originated somewhere around the Middle ages. In his journals Moorealan discussed some stories from the Black Death that he believed would evolve into the Westminster Shadow, tales of a strange beast, seen stalking the dark corners of the world, watching people.

The presence of the Shadow is said to draw in the darkness, to make a place cold and unwelcoming, to make it feel… disconnected from the real world. Oddly, however, its interactions with the world seem limited to acts of petty vandalism and mischief.

As well as his interference on the Underground extension, the Shadow has variously been blamed for broken windows, rearing horses, locked doors, stuttering gas supplies, and all manner of objects throwing themselves across the room.

Around the Great War, as interest in the worlds beyond our own peaked, there was a sharp increase in reports of the Shadow.

By the Blitz he had become a joke, with Tommy Philpott regularly noting on his Radio Half Hour: 'Even the Westminster Shadow has been taking a pop at the bombers,' before describing what unusual objects had (apparently) been thrown at the aircraft that week, ranging from 'those 'orrible curtains from number sixty three', to 'Churchill's spare breakfast'.

Eventually, after the second world war, sightings would fade way, to a sporadic trickle, as the shadow seemed to hibernate, until woken by the Underground extension.

A typical story of the Shadow, from its heyday between the wars, is included in the stage memoirs of John Pillbox, 'He Wore Moonboots' when discussing the bachelor Uncle, with whom he spent most summers when released from his expensive boarding school:

Uncle Rudolph was a good man, in all the ways that I now wish I could have appreciated at the time: he was kind, patient, and forgiving to a fault, talking to me like an adult, never hiding the truth, or spinning the little lies everybody else felt the need to wrap around my life like cotton wool.

To a young lad eager to fill his summer with mischief and adventure, he seemed dull, and boring, to the point of being a punishment. I longed to be on tour with my father, to be living out of hotels, and exploring back stage of the studios or theatres, not in a comfortable and steady home.

Rudolph was the white sheep of the family, turning his back on the arts, or self-indulgent academia, to study law, and invest himself in worthwhile endeavours. He was typical of the Clan Pillbox, in that he was rangy, lean, and cursed with the family conk. Unlike anybody else in my family tree he was… a grey man, without passion or colour, in his life, his manner, or clothes.

I did not think he had the family spark at all, at least until he told me one story, on Christmas Eve, as we sat by the roaring fire, in the company of my family.

"Go on Rudy," my mother said. "Tell your story."

Rudolph looked at me, as though he was unsure, as he swirled his whiskey in his glass and leant forwards.

"Well, a long time ago, when I was in a very junior role in the firm, and still wet behind the ears, I was sent by Old Mutton to deal with one of our clients, the landlord of an office building in the city. He was worrying about some of his tenants, some nice old ladies running some small concern, that kept insisting the neighbours in the other offices on their floor were making intolerable noise, banging, crashing, and throwing their furniture at the door. Trout Smith, the landlord was sure there was some game being played. The ladies were his only tenants on that floor, you see, and to his mind, they must be playing some kind of game to worm something out of their contracts."

I freely confess, there was something about the strain behind his voice, and the darkness in his eyes, that I would never have expected, from him.

"Well," Rudolph continued. "I went to the city, and to the building, up to the fifth floor to speak to the old ladies myself. I thought myself a smart enough whip. If the ladies were dishonest, I was confident I could sniff it out and expose them, or if they were honest, I hoped I could reason with them, to mediate a compromise. Trout follows me up, and looms in the doorway as I speak to the women, and... the first thing I notice is that their despair is all too real. They flustered at the thought of solicitors being involved and insisted that all they wanted was Trout to please talk to their neighbour, to kindly ask for... a little moderation in his... tempers. Well, Trout explodes with his usual insistence that they have no neighbours."

He paused to draw a breath, and to steel himself for the next part of the story.

"The women are adamant that somebody has been in that office. They said they saw his shadow in the frosted glass of the door, every day. That they heard him stomping about. Trout was every bit as adamant that they must have been wrong. So... we went to look for ourselves, and sure enough, the suite was empty, and unfurnished. There was no sign of the dust on the floor having been disturbed in months. We left footprints as we stepped inside. Trout was of course smirking and victorious. The women were... confused, and their expressions broke my heart. I tried to be kind, but Trout being Trout, he had to raise his voice, and warn the women he would not be taken in by their lies, or games, and¬ BOOM!"

Rudolph stamped his foot so hard, and so suddenly I almost escaped out through my own bowels!

"Boom! Something hit the wall behind us so hard that the whole room shook. I could feel it through my feet. I could see the dust leaping from the floor, and settling once more, obscuring our footprints. BOOM! It struck again, loud enough to make Trout squeak, and the women yelp, and I froze, looking around. BOOM! The light fitting crashed to the floor. And then... then I saw it... a shadow stretching out from under the door, flowing over the tiles like a liquid, and crawling up the wall, slithering into the form of... not a man... but neither a beast. Man like, I suppose, with bat wings, and a beaked head, and... a darkness that is richer and deeper than other shadows. It moved against the tide, flowing where the light from the window should have obliterated shadows. It spread out... And..."

"And?" Asked I, unsure if I really wanted to know the answer.

"And it swept its eyeless gaze over each of us, it stared at us, into our souls." Rudolph smiled, breaking the spell. *"Well, we retreated from that empty office, and I suggested that perhaps the Women may wish to relocate to another office on the floor above, where they would need not be quite so... alone. Trout's demeanour changed to honey and kindness in an instant, as he whimpered away. I got a friend from the clergy to visit him, and understand there was a blessing of the building, but I do believe that floor of his building remains empty."*

*

Although the Shadow is, as the name suggests, most active in Westminster, there have been alleged sightings throughout London, and often beyond. The most spot where the Shadow has most often been spotted used to be in a cobbled passageway, that is now the car park for a popular shopping centre in Westminster.

Dee and I spend our vigil in my car, watching the carpark over cups of coffee, and some music.

Around midnight, the carpark is almost empty.

My phone rings. It is Scamp, home from work and checking in.

I step out the car before I answer. "Hey."

"Hey!" Scamp says, bright but tired. "How's it going?"

"All quiet so far, how was work?"

"Oh, you know…" Scamp yawns. "I think I would rather have been bored with y¬"

A door slams, echoing through the car park, and making me jump out my skin.

In the same instant there is a crash on the other end of the phone, a cacophony of noise as all the pots in my kitchen leap off their hooks and hit the worktop.

Scamp yells in shock.

I whirl around.

The car park is empty.

I tell myself it was just a coincidence, all the way home, and spend a sleepless night holding my wife in a protective hug.

Part Two: Roads, Rails, And Canals.

When the last section of the M25 opened, in 1986, the motorway became the largest ring road in Europe. Circling Greater London, it connects to A Roads and motorways spurring off to every corner of mainland Britain, like a giant spiderweb.

The Capital is a transport hub. As well as the Thames offering access to the sea, it is threaded through with major roads, railways, and the Grand Union Canal, that was once the major artery of trade stretching from London to Birmingham, branching out to other cities on its way.

These transport routes have their own mythology, their own legends, and spectres.

Like any other city in the world, London has its share of ghostly hitchhikers who vanish in moving vehicles, black dogs that prowl the road, and strange figures that lurk at crossroads.

Slow Morris

Larry Crawley is a friendly, portly, man, with a mischievous smile, like a toby jug made flesh. He proudly wears a fleece and polo shirt, that both carry the logo for his company, Crawley Cab Tours. He talks freely as he drives.

"I used to be a cab driver, who ran guided walks on the side, you know?" He says, without looking back at us. "I had the leaflets in the back of the car there, for any takers, and it seemed natural to offer a driving tour, if people wanted it, and that really took off, to the point I was having to turn away airport runs because I had tours booked, and eventually, regular rides withered away in favour of the tours, so I threw myself all in with this side of my career, and boy… it's been a success, and a lot more fun."

Myself and Scamp are in the back of a taxicab, decorated in neon bright decals, offering insightful tours of London, themed around History, Mystery, Celebrity, or Ghosts. The leaflets in the back offer tours themed around Jack The Ripper, Moorealan and Retsim, or Royal London. There is another leaflet, that advertises the streaming channel for a group of paranormal investigators and ghost hunters.

We are currently merging with the M25.

Larry Crawley has a somewhat dubious honour, although it is sometimes misdescribed.

"According to the internet," he says, cheerfully, "I have seen Slow Morris more times than anybody else. I do not think that's true. There are people who use this motorway a lot more often than me, and they probably see him all the time, but don't recognise him for what he is. That's the thing. I recognised him more than others."

"Of course," Scamp says, "it helps that you have been actively hunting him."

"Spotting!" Larry corrects her. "I want to record his existence, and get the world to pay attention. Hunting suggests I'm out to kill him, or be rid of him."

Larry has been making regular expeditions around the M25, looking for the ghost called Slow Morris for some years now. His team of investigators have posted footage online, that is… suspiciously good, with clear views of what appears to be a living corpse driving an old white van.

If you believe the narration on the video, this is the best ever, unambiguous evidence of supernatural entities, ever produced.

If you don't, it's a really clever hoax that has gone viral, and caused a lot of discussion amongst special effects artists.

Larry looks over his shoulder at us. "You aren't believers, are you? It's okay. I know the signs. I won't hold it against you, but I will ask that you keep an open mind, if we see something."

Scamp raises an eyebrow at me.

I shrug.

We drive on, moving through the traffic.

Larry's plan is simple. He is going to drive in circles around the motorway, hoping he will pass the ghost, and be afforded an opportunity to catch it on the cameras rigged to the top of the car.

When we made contact with Larry, and arranged to be passengers on his spotting trip, I had no expectations of actually encountering the supernatural, but now I am not so sure. Although I am not yet ready to believe in a living corpse forever circling the motorway, like the Flying Dutchman of the road, Larry seems to genuinely believe it.

I am reminded of the controversy some years ago, the last time a bigfoot video made international headlines. The man who took the video was undoubtedly a true believer, but had occasionally 'spiced' the discussion with some manufactured evidence, fake footprints and videos, to build interest, and bring attention to the creatures he wanted to protect from hunters.

Somewhere, at the back of my mind, I wonder if Larry's videos are something similar.

It's not a pleasant thought, but it staves off the question I do not want to ask: If he wasn't faking the videos, what did he see?

*

The stories about Slow Morris disagree on several details, including who he was in life, or how he came to haunt the motorways of Britain. I say the motorways, because although most stories suggest he is forever orbiting London on the M25, there are some tales that have him straying far and wide. Indeed in some stories (fiercely defended by some as the original and true telling) he is forever trapped on the M1, at home at the opposite end of the country.

Stories began to spread online, around a decade ago. The earliest version I can find was picked up by a number of sites, after being posted from an anonymous source on a couple of forums:

So, I know you like weird stories, so here's mine:

Last week I was working night shift, on motorway patrol, with my mate Squeak. After a while we get told to respond to calls about some guy in an ancient van, driving recklessly, far too slowly, with his lights off. We thought we better pull him over for some wise words and advisory action.

Anyway, we go flying off round, with blue lights flashing, and our siren singing, but there is nobody there. We haven't passed anybody on the hard shoulder, or any vans going less than motorway speed, and we are too far from a junction for him to have gone anywhere.

Squeak chuckles, and says it must have been Slow Morris.

Of course, I don't believe him. Slow Morris is a legend in the force. The ghost of some old boy who ¬and believe me I know how this sounds¬ got in a scuffle with London's evil sorcerer Mister Retsim, forty years ago. The version I had was that Slow Morris almost run over Retsim, jumping a red light at a crossing. Whatever Morris said convinced Retsim that the mortal world would be better off without the driver, and cursed him, to be forever in a hurry, but forever slow, never to stop, and never to get... anywhere. Every now and again he will turn up, and make a nuisance of himself. By the time we get there, he is gone, vanished into the shadows, but... a few officers glimpsed him, and... the poor bugger is mummified, a dead body in a white van, trundling around, gathering more scratches and dents.

Now I'm not one to believe in ghost stories, so that leaves me one conclusion: that somebody is up to no good. So... I do some digging, and look at the CCTV, but here is the weird thing: the van is old, and I can't get a clear read on the numberplate, and it just vanishes between cameras.

It was a mystery with no way to solve it, so sometimes you just have to let it go, and move on... which I was doing pretty well at, until last night.

Last night I was getting a Herbert to breathe into my little tube, on the hard shoulder, when I heard the blare of horns. There were cars swerving around this van, trundling along, really, really, slowly. I got a glimpse of the driver, just a glimpse, on his way past.

It was a man, dried and shrivelled as a mummy, dressed in old clothes, with rotting teeth and dead eyes.

I caught a glimpse, but it was burned into my mind.

When he turned to look at me, it was with a look of absolute despair, pleading for help, but then... Then he just vanished.

Since Curtvile Moorealan's journals were published a whole swathe of odd stories have been attributed to Mister Retsim. Slow Morris is just one of the countless tales that used him as the magic machinery that allowed ghosts, and ghouls to exist. Many stories claim he is still wandering around, or was seen at some vague point in the past.

Slow Morris is just one of the fabled victims to have fallen foul of the magician.

There have been various attempts to identify Morris, by looking for a tradesman who vanished in a white van, after a potential incident. None of the arguments are convincing, and the endeavour seems in poor taste to me.

Not every telling includes Retsim. They do not include a near miss or accident to justify the curse, they simply describe Morris driving off, and never making it home, cursed for all time, without reason at all.

*

After three hours, our expedition is in its final stages, and Larry is heading for home.

We have not seen any sign of Morris.

"The traffic is going too well," Larry explains. "Morris tends to appears when there's a bit of congestion, and a few delays. You need a little anger and some tooting horns, to act as chum in the water."

Scamp gives me a look. Larry neglected to mention that before.

Before we can ask a question, there is a worrying noise from the engine, and a flashing light on the dashboard.

A few minutes later, the car is on the hard shoulder, and we are a safe distance up the embankment, as Larry calls for help on the phone.

Ten meters back down the shoulder is a bright orange rescue phone, that begins ringing.

Scamp laughs. "I guess traffic control can see us on the cameras."

I walk over. "I will let them know Larry has it all in hand."

The phone continues to ring, until I pop open the case, and lift the receiver. I am greeted by the hissy, scratchy, recording of the jaunty sea shanty.

"Hello?" My own voice asks. "Hello? I think you have the wrong number. This is a public phone."

My heart stops.

The world spins.

Somebody laughs, a tar thick, venomous sound.

I hang up.

"Hey!" Scamp shouts, plunging into the long grass and nettles of the embankment. "Hey! Look at these guys!"

She lifts up a cardboard box from the grass. Something is moving around inside. More than one something, small and furry.

Scamp pouts, her eyes wide and gooey. "Oh… hey little guys! Who left you here? Who could have left you here?"

"Scamp," I say, nervously, "that was…"

She shows me the box.

Two skeleton thin kittens huddle within, mewling and shivering.

"I need your coat," she says.

"Scamp!" I say, despairingly, as I shrug off my coat.

"What?" She asks, her expression softening. "What happened?"

I try my best to describe the phone call, as she gently swaddles the cats, and looks up a vet near our home on her phone.

Blackthorn

Grace and I are stood on a bridge over a lonely stretch of canal, in one of those corners of London where the sounds of the city, and the traffic feel distant, as though the city treats this tranquil corner, not far from a major railway terminal, with reverence.

The night is clear and cold, with a sky full of stars.

We watch the ink dark water, wondering what makes the occasional ripple under the milky streetlight.

My phone beeps.

It's a message from Scamp. A photo of Crackers and Jack, our newly adopted kittens, who are somehow perched atop the distribution board in the hallway again.

I show Grace, and she giggles.

"So cute!" She coos.

There is movement down by one of the locks.

Grace and I both turn to watch in a tense silence. In that moment, in that eerie stillness, with those velvet thick shadows, it is all too easy to imagine London's black lion emerging from the knotted weeds and skeletal trees.

A pair of burning green eyes catch the streetlight, and glow in the darkness.

Grace and I take a step back, together.

Something growls in the darkness.

*

Blackthorn is one of the newest of the Unearthly stories. Grace first stumbled on the story a few days ago, when one of the local newspapers picked up the story. Tellingly, for a tale of the Unearthly, the paper had not interviewed any witnesses to the alleged sighting, instead reporting the 'popular tale going viral on social media', with the same blurry photographs that could be found around the internet.

The earliest version of the story I could track was from an anonymous account (HermitIX) that posted the same block of text seven times, in various groups, before closing down and vanishing.

The story lived on, picking up traction and quickly going viral, growing as it was garnished and embellished. This is the original version, before some of the more colourful aspects developed:

I have just had the scariest experience of my life.

I was walking my dog along the towpath at Cushing's Lock, when all of a sudden my dog stops walking, and starts barking at something across on the other bank. I crouched down to calm her, and was getting really worried when something roared back.

It emerged from the shadows on the far side, and it was... impossible to think of how I couldn't see it before. It was a lion, a jet black lion, with fur like tar, and eyes like embers. It must have been about the size of a horse.

For a few moments I had no idea what to do, so I just crouched there and shivered, until it turned, snapped up a fox, a whole fox, in its jaws, and walked away.

I have never walked home quicker.

For a while I was terrified to try and report it, as nobody would believe me, but my BIL (a policeman) says that the lion is well known, and has been for years and years. His name is Blackthorn, and he was imported to be an exotic pet for a millionaire in Kensington, but when he realised he was going to be raided, he drove it to the Heath, and released it, thinking it would be caught in a few days, but wouldn't be traced back to him.

As it happens, he was exactly wrong. The police knew he had the animal, and easily found the evidence to charge him, but were never able to find the lion, and now it lives in the wild, living off wild vermin, and feral strays.

The most interesting part of this story is that since it went viral, countless other sightings, dating back to when the lion was (allegedly) released on the Heath have been shared, all claiming a long history of sightings, but all of them undoubtedly being shared for the first time, in recent days.

They very quickly cemented into a linear narrative, a mythos for Blackthorn.

Sightings of Alien Big Cats are not uncommon across the UK. In the Southeast they have been regularly reported in Kent and Sussex, where they can be convincingly lost in the Downs, the Weald, and the countryside the stories sometimes supported by photographs, or slain sheep.

In other, more remote corners of the country, in the Highlands of Scotland, the Yorkshire Moors, and Dartmoor, they are positively flourishing, with long histories of reports, and countless encounters.

However, most of these reports suggest animals that are more akin to a large Kellas cat, or a small black leopard, a far cry from a giant lion.

Blackthorn is also unusual in his, apparently, going unnoticed deep in an urban setting. Even with London's heathlands and parks, it seems difficult to believe that an unusually large lion, or the victims of its vast appetite, might have gone unnoticed for a matter of years.

The manner of his appearance, or rather his supernatural disappearance, does call to mind far more established tales of the Unearthly: those of the demonic black dogs that have long been said to stalk the roads and churchyards of Britain, bringers of ill omen and dark tiding, said to have left their mark in the local folklore of many counties.

There is another coincidence, that I have tried to ignore, afraid of imbuing it with undeserved significance.

In his journals, Moorealan records a list of thirteen tales of giant black dogs, from around the British Isles, recounting each tale in considerable detail, and his own grandly gothic style. He then persuades Mister Retsim to help him glimpse one such creature. The journals embark on a flight of fancy where Moorealan and Retsim both engage in a ritual, hidden in a barge at Cushing's Lock, to thin the veil and allow them a glimpse at the guardians who stalk between worlds.

Moorealan describes an ink-dark creature, the size of a shire horse, and as much like a lion as he was like a dog, but truly belonging to neither family.

*

The cat that steps out of the shadows, growling at us, is black, but is a scrawny little shorthair cat. Its husky growl echoes around the canal.

Grace breaks into relieved laughter, and gives me a playful shove.

My heart remember to beat, as I draw a breath.

Another cat steps onto the towpath, and another…and another… Very quickly there is a small army, filling the path, all of them staring our way, and growling.

Grace takes my hand, as we back away.

Somebody whistles behind us.

I almost jump out of my skin. When I look around, there is a man with a scruffy beard, and dark eyes, in a raggedy and threadbare overcoat, and a shapeless hat, leaning on a cane.

The old man whistles a jaunty sea shanty, the same shanty from those bizarre phone calls, and immediately the cats trot over the bridge, straight between Grace and I, in single file, and follow the man into the overgrown embankment, vanishing into the shadows.

I stare after them.

Grace looks at me, and mouths three words. *What. The. Actual?*

I answer her with a helpless look.

The Grey Lady Of Arden Junction

Dee wakes me around two. "Hey! I'm getting something!"

"Ugh!" Grace moans, on the backseats of my car, wrapping her pillow over her head.

This is perhaps the sixth or eighth time tonight that Dee has reported an unusual spike on her infrasound detector. She shows me the screen, and the levels are high, chattering away through the frequencies.

I nod at her, grab the camera Scamp has loaned me, and step out of my car into the cold of the night.

Strictly speaking we are out of bounds tonight, outside London, and just beyond the M25, inside of Essex. I am parked on the overbridge for lonely country road, that spans a dual carriageway, just before it joins the M25 at a new junction, completed less than a year ago.

The motorway is a band of light, afire against the horizon.

Down in the cutting, the dual carriageway is quiet, and almost still, the traffic reduced to a sparse trickle at this time in the morning, but never gone completely.

Dee stands a little further down the bridge, holding out her meter. Her face furrows.

I sweep the carriageways with my camera, but can't see anything.

*

The current sightings of the Grey Lady began while the new A Road and the new motorway junction were being constructed. Security guards, left to protect the plant and materials at night reported a figure standing in the middle of the freshly lain carriageways.

At first the police concluded that what had been seen was loose plastic sheeting, flapping in the wind.

Then one of their officers claims to have seen the trespasser and given chase, only for the stranger, a woman dressed in a grey hood and drab skirts, vanished, apparently through a solid fence.

The stretch of road in question was built over wasteland, unsuitable for other development. The mouldering ruins of Arden House, damaged beyond repair in the war, and left to rot, and growing ever more dangerous since, were raised to the ground, to make way for the development.

The grounds of Arden House had long been said to be haunted by the ghost of a woman in grey and a hood, looking to steal a few moments with her beloved, just as she had in life. Until the house was abandoned in the war, these stories, and sightings were common.

In the 1960s, the stage magician and children's entertainer, Corbet Soot, investigated the Grey Lady, for his series 'In A Sceptical Light'.

The episode, filmed in black and white, offers one of the few glimpses of the manor as it had been, half crumbling away, and shrouded in mist, the gothic brickwork stained by years of rain, and veiled in ivy.

Indeed, the episode does feature a shadowy shape, drifting across the overgrown gardens in the distance, but is quickly explained, as Soot and his team dig down through the gardens and find an underground stream.

The ghost, it seemed, was no more than a column of midges, following the buried stream. At a distance, the swarm of insects appeared as a half-solid object, woven from shadow, that could, with your hairs prickling on the back of your neck, be interpreted as the Grey Lady.

Could the same explanation apply to the new sightings?

We know from the planning and construction records that the stream was contained and protected, beneath the road, and that the road was built up in a way that makes it unlikely, but not impossible.

However, the sightings are most often seen at night, in autumn or winter, when the insects would be expected to be less active.

The way I see it is this: Midges exist, where as ghosts, at best *may* exist, which puts the insect, as an unlikely suspect, but one which remains far more likely than an otherworldly presence.

*

"Guys?" Grace says, from the car.

Dee and I look back.

Grace points at something above us. "What's that?"

We look up.

There is a light above the horizon, it seems to be hovering over the M25, but I have no way to judge the distance. It could a satellite in orbit, a jet, or it could be a star, far out in the endless gulf of space.

I bring up the camera, and snap a rapid flurry of photographs, trying to follow the light.

The light moves, it swoops down over the dual carriageway, casting a ethereal blue light over the trees on the embankment. It is so low that the handful of cars and trucks on the carriageway slam on their brakes and swerve to avoid the ball of hazy blue light that zooms under the bridge, and… never emerges on the other side.

Grace rushes grab Dee, they are both shaking.

I look at the pictures I took.

They show a blob of light over the road, the blue light painting the embankments and the bridge.

My hands are trembling.

*

A few days later I am putting the finishing touches to dinner, in the kitchen, as Scamp is in the living room of our little house, with Dee and Grace, pouring the wine, and watching the viral dashcam footage of the Arden Road Object.

The footage has been picked up by countless news sites, and an interview with one of the drivers has been shown all over the place, picked up by a number of late night chat shows and comedians, on bot sides of the Atlantic.

Dee has been interviewed a few times too, doing her best to plug the upcoming podcast as she goes, carefully describing what we did see. People keep asking if what she saw was a UFO, or is she believes its is a ghost, or a hoax.

Dee consistently offers the same answer: "I don't know what I saw. I am sorry that is not the answer you want, but to me it is a bigger, better, scarier, and far, far, more beautiful answer. I don't know. It's exciting not to know. It means we get to find out."

Already the supernova of attention is beginning to fade.

I am plating up, as the phone rings.

Scamp grabs the phone, and frowns. "They hung up."

A few seconds later it rings again.

Scamp snatches it up.

The line is dead once more.

It rings a third time.

I pick up the handset.

The same jaunty sea shanty plays, scratchy and broken. Then it comes to an end, and a voice at the other end screams, loud, raw, and bloodcurdling, a primordial cry of pain and terror, loud enough for the kittens to scamper away and hide behind the sofa, loud enough for the others to look up and stare at me.

"Please," a voice at the other end of the line begs, "please, no… no…"

It screams again.

My heart stops and my stomach twists in a knot.

The voice is… my voice. Sobbing, broken, and rasping, but… mine nevertheless.

We did not know then, that such calls were going to become a regular nuisance at homw.

Neale Lane Station

There are several abandoned, disused, or incomplete stations scattered around London.

Neale Lane is a surface station for the Underground, built in the thirties, the final decoration was never completed, and the station never opened. It was a victim of economics. Budgets were strained, and it was deemed that the adjustments to service, the running costs and staffing, of Neale Lane, and other stations like it, were an expense that could bot be afforded. Instead, it and its sister stations were simply locked up, and left.

Today the station is still locked and sealed.

Scamp and I are sitting in my car, watching the rain, nursing our coffees, waiting for the caretaker who will allow us to access the rarely seen platform.

This is the first time we have worked on the podcast for some months, and it is a welcome respite from our 'real' lives. The last few months have been hard.

Since my encounter at Arden Junction, the strange telephone call, with the scratchy music, and the imitation of my own screaming voice, have been a constant irritation and harassment. We have gone ex-directory, changed our number, and changed our mobile numbers, we have even started using call screening, but still it calls for me, from a withheld number that has not yet been tracked.

These days we hear it in the voicemail, over and over, day after day.

We have sought help from the police, and legal help, but somehow it is there. Even if we no longer take the damned calls, and skip through them, deleting them, as we check our voicemail for relevant messages, just knowing they are there sends a shiver down my spine.

Between dealing with the cursed calls, Christmas, New Years, and the constant grind of our day jobs, the winter has been long, and exhausting. Even when we finally had the time to work on the podcast, synchronising our schedules with Dee and Grace was a nightmare, and having the energy to take on more work was a rare luxury.

But, at last, here we are.

Scamp keeps checking her phone, watching our cats in the nanny-cam, not out of worry, but because their playful mischief is always amusing.

A white van pulls up, and Nisha Rani, the caretaker, hops out, in her high-vis all weather coat, and waves us over. We have to don high visibility vests and hard hats, before she can unlock the security gates, and show us in to the station.

We walk through the bare shell of a lobby and down onto the platforms. The unfinished space has a bare, industrial feel. The platforms are securely fenced off from the open lines, making it feel gloomy and shadowy. There is the iron framework of a canopy, but no glass, so the drizzle fills the platform.

Miss Rani flashes us a grin. "If you are looking into the stories, you have to imagine how this looked late at night, without the fencing up. Imagine being on the train, slowing to a stop at the signal down there." She points to a red light visible through the fence. "Your train stops at a platform you never noticed before, that isn't on the tube map, that looks… wrong. The doors of the train don't open, and maybe you see somebody moving around back here… back before our workers were required to dress from head to toe in high visibility clothes. It would be easy to convince yourself you had seen something… strange."

I have to agree that the station lends itself to stories of the Unearthly.

It's gloomy and shadowy, the sounds of traffic muffled and distant, the quiet broken by the rumble of passing trains.

Scamp points at the heavy doors in the yellow brick wall. "What are those?"

Miss Rani gestures at a couple, with warning signs on. "Plant rooms. I can't show you those because of the equipment within, but you can see the washrooms, and the waiting room."

"We'll take the waiting room," Scamp says, looking at me. "You can check the loos."

Of course.

I ease open the door, and step into the disused gent. It is dank, cold, and echoey, with old fashioned sinks, and stalls that have been undisturbed for some years.

I step into the room, and look around.

Something moves in the corner of my eye.

*

The fences were erected in 2002, after a passenger tried to leave the train while it was stopped at signal. The internet quickly decided it was for more…supernatural reasons.

One story shared online around that time read:

The real reason for the fences will be obvious to some.

They don't want us to see the ghosts.

I have been on a train that has stopped by Neale Lane Station many times over the years, and I never like it, because I always remember that ONE time… The one time I saw them… the dead people. Most of the rest of the people on the train didn't notice, but I heard a few gasps, and confused discussions, so some of the others did.

The dead were stood at the back of the cutting, wearing old clothes, really old clothes, like they were from some other age, hundreds of years old, with those weird collars... The people were grey, and rotting, skeletons with just patches of skin hanging off them, and brown teeth, hollow eyes, and sickly boils and sores all over.

They dragged themselves forwards in lurching, stumbling steps, and one was reaching out for the window, when at last the train moved.

The way I see it, if a few of us could see the ghosts on that train, and a few more on another, and another... sooner or later there will be enough whispers of the dead to spur this kind of action. There is no way THEY want to admit what is going on at that station, so they create a story about a wayward passenger wanting to skip off the train.

I can find no evidence of stories about ghosts at the station before the fences were put up, but they sprouted rapidly, like weeds, after, flourishing for a few years, then waning away quickly.

There was a brief rekindling of interest in 2009, when a popular ghost hunting TV show was refused permission to hold a séance based investigation of the platforms. Once again, speculation of what was being hidden ran wild (in reality, there were engineering works ongoing, the essential renewals of power and distribution equipment).

Tales of the dead being seen at the station are consistent.

Animated corpses, from varying centuries, and varying fancy dress, are seen on the platform, in huddled groups. They are always described as ashen, grey, rotting, and mummified, with brown teeth and an infestation of open sores and pustules.

They always claim to be some years old, and some even claim to be clippings from old newspapers, but this is always a fiction. None of the stories can be verified, none of the reports existed, and none of them have any trace before the fences were put up.

*

The washrooms are empty.

I turn and walk back out onto the platform.

Scamp glares at me. "Where have you been? We were looking for you!" She prods me with a finger. "Did you… did you hide from us? We looked in there! Did you think this was funny?"

I give her a helpless look. "What?"

Her expression hardened. "Where were you?"

"I just…" I shook my head. "It's been about two minutes. I walked in, looked around, and…"

Scamp grabs me. "I was scared! You idiot!"

Part Three: Green And Pleasant Corners

Upwards of forty percent of London is designated as "Green Space". With parks, heathland, commons, and more than eight million trees, Greater London is one of the world's largest urban forests. One church in Totteridge, High Barnet, boasts a yew tree that is conservatively estimated to be over one thousand years old, but is likely twice that age. It was certainly there when Doomsday Book was written, and could have been there before the Romans invaded.

These green spaces are remnants of the market towns and rural communities that were consumed and assimilated as London grew outwards into the vast metropolis that we now recognise.

They also offer a fantastic illusion.

With populations of deer, wildflowers, woodpeckers and bluebells, they take on the timeless serenity of the countryside, and it is easy to feel that you have travelled far from the city.

It is very easy to believe that nature plays by different rules here.

The Beast Of Bushy Park

Archie Rhys, London's second most popular Drive Time DJ, is a round faced, bubbly, New Zealander, full of laughter and smiles, with bright eyes, and a rubbery, expressive face. According to the press kit his agent supplied, he came to London sixteen years ago to spend a few months performing in Panto, but ended up staying indefinitely as an institution of the airwaves.

The man who meets Grace and I for coffee by the glistening emerald pond is very different from the man who brings chaos and the any-request-playlist to commuters enduring the rush hour, and it isn't just because he is a clean cut kind of handsome, without his trademark wild hair, safari shirt, and cravat. It's his soft tone, and the thoughtful way he considers his answers before he speaks.

"So," he says, with a smile. "Where do you want to start?"

Grace sets the recorder running. "How about you tell us about the show, first?"

"Ah!" He nods. "Well, the show was Urban Nature, and it was our fifth season in 2012. My job was to basically be the interested idiot, the guy with about the same level of understanding as the viewers, who the experts, the naturalists and the zoologists, could explain things to. There were mini-shows through the week, filling the gaps where the shows imported from America were only forty five minutes long, without adverts. Then at the end of the week we had our hour long live show. I was deep in the park, with an outside broadcast van, set up to watch the park's deer, and was waiting for my cue to start my spiel, once a VT, a video taped insert, was running. You know the sort of thing, a little pre-recorded bit on what a Royal Park is, or the history of the bandstand, or…something. Anyway, with a few seconds to go to air, there is chattering from the crew because they can see this figure lurking in the background, and they think some prankster is about ready to crash into our feed… Which is something that had happened a few times over the years. A production assistant went running out, and couldn't find them, so we went outside, and I am stood there, near the van, with the view behind me, smiling at my camera man, and they count me down, and… I launch into it."

Archie shivers.

Grace looks at him. "Are you okay?"

He nods. "I'm talking about the deer we have seen during the day, and we cut to some of the footage we caught through the day. I hear this weird noise from the shadows. And I admit, I am thinking it's going to be a hoaxer, so I ignore it. Then I glimpse the thing, and I laugh, and tell the other hosts that I'm sorry if I seem distracted but some student in a gorilla suit is lurking around, I am hoping they aren't going to make a fool out of us. Then I carry on, and as we cut to the next film of the deer this…*thing*… bursts from the trees, knocks over Bill the camera man, smashing his camera, and vanishes into the shadows. And… it isn't a student in a suit. It's big, and leathery, wearing grey furs, with eyes like an octopus than a man, and with a jaw that opens to reveal… too many teeth, and all of them sharp. It screeches, and it smashes the camera, and it is gone. Gone! And…" He rubs his face. "And they don't cut back to me, they talk about technical difficulties, and… I'm warned to avoid talking about it for at least seven years, but… When somebody else spilled the beans, and was being called a hoaxer, I thought I should come clean about it." He sighs. "And the truth is, a lot of people aren't going to believe it. They will put this down to being one of my wacky stories, but… it was out there. I don't know what it was, or where it went, why nobody else cares its out there, but… there is something that likes the peace and quiet of this park, and it didn't much like the noise and bustle of camera crews and snaking cables. You know?"

Archie is an awkward spot. The story was reported in the press three years ago, when a producer included it in his memoirs. The story was picked up as a footnote in the national press, and there was a petition for the broadcaster to turnover any unused footage that might offer a glimpse at the strange ape-like creature.

The broadcaster claimed no images were found.

Archie has no evidence to support his story, but is clearly not lying. Whatever he saw, he truly believes it was something that could not have been a man in a suit.

His fear is absolutely genuine.

"I don't know what I saw," he tells us. "If it was a hoax, then it convinced me. If it wasn't… then it is a genuine mystery, and you have to admit, that is kind of exciting, isn't it"

The Walthamstow Object

The Wren Waters Nature Reserve is one of London's best little secrets. The sprawling wetlands contain the reservoirs that supply millions of Londoners, shrouded in grassland and wild habitats, that have encouraged a thriving population of birds, insects, and animals. As well as bird watchers, the Reserve is popular with cyclists, walkers, and families.

An old railway embankment runs through the park, giving a raised platform from which birdwatchers can look down on the flats and waters, offering a wonderful, and unique, vantage point.

One nook of the reserve is visible from the balcony of Cedric Jenkins' apartment in St Michael's Tower, a nineteen sixties' vintage concrete tower block, given a recent facelift by shiny new ceramic cladding.

Jenkins' is a retired insurance assessor, once sporty, but now frail and a little doddery, relying on a walking frame, to show us from the door to his balcony.

Scamp borrows his kitchen to make a pot of tea, while I help Jenkins settle on his little bench. He has a set of binoculars, and a cheap camera, with a cumbersome zoom lens, on the bench beside him.

"Are you a birdwatcher?" I ask.

Jenkins tries to both nod, and shake his head, at once. "Well, yes, but… that is more a result, than the cause."

A penny drops for me. "You are waiting for it to come back?"

Jenkins wants to shake his head, but can't. Instead he smiles. "Well, if it ever does… I'll make damn sure I catch it. There are a lot of people who laughed at me, who won't laugh this time."

I turn and look out over the Wren Park.

The long grass is painted silver with frost, set afire by the low winter sun.

I help Jenkins get warm in a blanket. "You know, we could talk in¬"

"No!" He chuckles. "There is no need. I am quite used to it. I prefer it out here."

Scamp steps out with the pot of tea.

When we are all settled, Jenkins points to a path, emerging from the trees, deep in the wetlands. "That's where I was. Almost a year ago now." He sighs. "I was a bit more active back then, and used to get off the bus down there, and follow that path across the Wetlands. It wasn't much of a shortcut, but it was a nice enough walk. I did it every day, and not once did I ever see anything like… it."

Scamp nods, encouraging him. "So… what did you see?"

Jenkins pauses. "Well, it wasn't so much what I saw, at first. It was the sound, like a steam whistle, right in the middle of my skull, so sharp and loud it made me feel like my teeth were about to crack. I staggered out of the trees, and looked up, and that was when I saw it."

"It?" Scamp asks.

"A disc of silver," Jenkins says, "about as wide as bus is long, but not as tall as a bus. The surface rippled like a liquid. It twisted, caught the sun, and…was suddenly too bright to look at, and I was falling upwards." He clicks his fingers. "And just like that I was coming around in hospital, hurting all over, and on a drip."

*

There is something of Jenkins' story that he can't tell.

There were nine days between Jenkins leaving his office, taking the bus, and claiming to have seen the object, and his waking up in hospital. A lot happened in those nine days, which is almost as interesting as what had not happened.

Around the time that Jenkins was last seen, air traffic controllers around London did detect a large unidentified vessel in London's airspace, and fighter jets were scrambled to investigate, but saw nothing. An atmospheric effect was blamed.

It is also worth noting that despite the wetlands, and the sky, being overlooked by a tower block, journalists covering the story were not able to find a single witness, who saw the object, at least while the story was the air traffic controllers' strange contact.

Witnesses did come forwards eventually, after Jenkins' description had been published.

Jenkins was missing for six days, before he was found on a Scottish beach, dehydrated, and suffering terrible sunburn across much of his body. He was unconscious, and unresponsive, for another three days before he came too. Two of his teeth were missing, and he had three healed breaks, that Jenkins denies any knowledge of.

There was a fresh scar in his right armpit, that has never been explained.

After Jenkins' story reached the newspapers, a lot of people came forwards, claiming to have seen the object, either over London, or over the Scottish coast, near Edinburgh, around the time Jenkins was being returned.

The story is most commonly shared by those claiming it to have been aliens, although Jenkins never used that word himself. Indeed, he told me that he hates the word, he thinks it instantly discredits his experiences, and will sour his chances of ever finding the truth.

*

Jenkins is of course, not the only person who has seen something odd over the skies of London. In fact, his is the best known story of a minor flap, which is to say the best known encounter in a short flurry of sightings, that lasted for about six months.

In that span, there were a number of videos uploaded to social media, that seemed to show mushroom shaped craft, with a honeycombed surface of a slate grey metal, drifting over parks and heaths across London. These were, at the time, largely thought to be hoaxers using helium filled balloons, piloted by a small remote controlled vehicle.

There were several sightings of men in some kind of foil anti-contamination suits, apparently watching picnickers in various parks, lurking in the shadows and the treelines. A few photographs offered a little weight to these stories, but they too were put down to student hoaxers.

Then things took a dangerous turn, as aircraft approaching Britain's major airports started reporting near misses with men wearing silver space suits, and some kind of jetpack. These incidents received interest from the press, and may well have primed the atmosphere to be receptive to Jenkin's story.

In Bromley park, a local playgroup having their teddy bear's picnic broke into hysterics as the children reported being stalked and harasses by small men with no face, that vanished into a "rocket made of water". Some of those children also claimed to have seen a large circle of metal hanging above the park.

The adults saw nothing, but were reportedly disturbed by the genuine terror, and consistent descriptions, of the children.

Then, some months after Jenkins' experiences, police forces around the country received a spate of reports from motorists on the M25 and M11, of large blue lights flying over the motorways, and turning so bright, that they almost caused accidents.

No explanation was ever given for these encounters.

*

"They did deliberately, you know?" Jenkins tells us. "The Government. They planted all those stories about aliens and spaceships. I saw something that nobody was meant to, and…they made sure I could never tell my story without being laughed at and bullied."

Scamp gives me a look.

"You…" I clear my throat. "Why do you think it was the government?"

"Logistics," Jenkins says. "It is a question of who has the resources, for the… experiment, and for the coverup after."

Scamp shows him one of my photographs from Arden Junction. "I don't suppose it looked like this?"

Jenkins considers the photograph and frowned.
"What's that meant to be?"

I shrug. "We have no idea."

I shrug. "We have no idea."

The Other London

We have another story to investigate while we are in the neighbourhood.

Scamp and I enter Wren park, and follow the main path, along the foot of the railway embankment. Branches of the path peel away through each of the bridges and tunnels. We ignore the most used arches, and walk to a smaller arch, for a narrow foot passage.

Scamp gives me a look as we stand, watching the fishermen on the far side of the passage. She smiles. "Well, that still looks like our London on the other side."

"Should I?" I ask.

She takes my hand, and we walk through the passage. It is full of echoes, that make our breathing too loud, and out footfalls linger.

We emerge on the far side, to find the city exactly as we left it.

The footpath loops away, and we take the scenic route back.

*

Six days earlier, we are in Pluckley in Kent.

Jim Roland is behind the bar. The jovial landlord is big and burly, with a permanently furrowed brow and a square jaw. He invites us into the function room to interview him.

"It was a long time ago," he warns us, "and you know how the memory plays tricks, but… I am happy to talk if you want."

"How old were you?" I ask.

He shrugs. "Fifteen, I think. Maybe sixteen?"

"So…" I look at him. "Are you okay to tell the story?"

"Well, it was early morning, and I was on my way to school, in no real rush to get there, and cutting through Wren Park risked getting muddy, but shaved some time off my journey, so I took the path through, and used the passageway that we all knew as Squeezegut, with my headphones in, minding my own business, enjoying my own little world, when suddenly the tape snarls and shrieks. So I stop the tape, and look at my player, and its fine, the tape is working fine, but the music sounds like its playing at half speed. I guess the batteries are dead, so I tuck it in my pocket, and keep walking, and halfway under the bridge, it feels like…the air is too thick, like I'm walking through treacle, and the light flickers."

He pauses to draw breath.

I wait for him to go on.

"And…" He shudders. "And when I step out the far end, everything was wrong. The grass, the trees, and reeds were all gone. There was churned mud, and the water was dark and skanky. The sky was brown, a sort of khaki brown, choked with fumes, and the smell… the smell was overpowering. At first I thought the mountain that filled the lake was spoiled meat, like a landfill, but then I saw the faces, and the limbs, and realised it was people. Dead people. They were broken, and loose, like ragdolls, skeletal thin, and mottled with sores and rashes. There was a rumble, the deep throaty sound of diesel engines, and I turned to look back, and… trains were up on the embankment, tipping these wagons, one at a time, spilling more bodies down the embankment, and people with bulldozers were at the bottom of the bank, shoving them into the lake, into the pile, while other men, all in overalls, gasmasks, and hard hats, were spraying the pile with hoses. Anyway, one of the me saw me, and he pointed at me, shouting, and there were others, wearing green overalls, like…olive and camouflage, with the same hard hat and gas masks, but they had rifles, and they came running at me. Well, I turned back, and ran through the passage faster than I ever ran, and almost made it to the entrance before I heard these loud cracks. Guns… didn't sound like they did on TV, and maybe it was the echo in the passage, but they blotted out all the other sound. Something hit me here…"

Roland unbuttons his shirt, and pulls it open, to show us the knot of scar tissue on his collar bone.

"They shot you?" Scamp asks, her eyes wide.

Roland nods. "It hit me like a sledgehammer, and I stumbled out, back into the real world, into the daylight, the grass, the park, and I ran blindly, all the way to the main road, before I fell in front of a passing car, that thankfully, stopped. Then I passed out."

Roland was rushed to the hospital, where he was found to be already suffering not only from the gunshot wound, but from a terrible fever and strange infection. One of the doctors that treated him, and the driver of the car he stopped, all fell deathly ill with the same fever that day, and it was only through luck, that the driver had been on his way home from a nightshift, so had not met anybody else, that the authorities were able to implement a quarantine, and prevent further infection.

The bacterial infection was never identified, and thankfully, has not been seen again.

"They said," Roland continues, "that my memory, my perception, was skewered by the fever, and the shock, and the blood loss, but… What else explains it? Where else could I have gone, other than another time, and place, to our future, that explains the being shot, and the infection, and… everything." He taps his lips. "I think the needle skipped on reality, and I sort of blipped a long way ahead, to where we might still be headed, and… I lay awake some nights, wondering how many others get blipped, and never make it back. How many people just… vanish." He rubs his face. "And the way I see it, I'm lucky, because the whole world is still moving, isn't it. Spinning, and rolling around the sun. I'm lucky I ended up in the same place *on Earth*, because if I ended up in the same place *in space,* I might have been… adrift in empty space, while the Earth was weeks, or months, away, you know?"

I measure my tone, carefully. "You are convinced that it was real? You will never consider it might have been… the results of your condition?"

Roland stares at me. "Never. I know what I saw. I know what happened."

We talk a little longer, and gather more material, then head home.

In the car, Scamp wears one of her thoughtful frowns. "You heard the way he talked about the bodies. What does that remind you of?"

I shudder. "I don't know. A plague pit?"

"Neale Lane," Scamp says. "The dead people, that were supposed to be seen on the platform."

She has a point.

"It could be a coincidence," I warn her.

"Yeah," she agrees. "But... it's weird, right?"

Part Four: Mirror Mirror

When the Unearthly London column was running in the magazine, my first piece on Mirror People, or Peeping Blurs, generated far more feedback, in the letter pages and on the web, than any other piece in the magazine.

Even after my columns had run their course, Peeping Blurs were a regular fixture in the letters page for six further months, and even today, I have occasional readers tracking me down on social media, to share their experiences with me.

When planning the podcast it quickly became apparent that this was topic too big to fit into a segment of one of the themed episodes, and would instead require an episode of its own, and even then, the few stories we could select would offer only a *suggestion* of the mystery.

I have tried to select stories that are generally representative of the larger mystery, but please keep in mind, that these are very much the tip of the iceberg.

The Cartmel Prediction

Curtvile Moorealan once wrote: "Few stories have the good sense to start at the beginning."

Most coverage of the Peeping Blurs will begin with the first incident to be reported in the news: the spate of sightings disturbing year seven at Aldred Road School, but that was not where the story began. The truth is, tens of thousands of us, all across the country, were part of the story's beginning, and none of us realised, until decades later.

I was ten years old, in Year Six, the last year of Primary School, when the Cartmel Prediction was finally confirmed.

In 1973, Professor Drew Cartmel had been studying the Noel Cascade, the beautiful meteor shower that is visible in the penultimate week of December, every year, as the Earth spins through a river of cosmic debris, some of which burns in the atmosphere as it succumbs of the Earth's gravity.

Cartmel's analysis of the debris suggested that the unusual electric blue hue of the meteors was caused by a cocktail of rare metals burning. His model of the size and orbit of the object suggested something roughly the size of Paris, that would pass close enough to Earth to be observed every six thousand years.

It was decades later that astronomers detected the object on course to intercept within days of Cartmel's predicted appearance.

The object caught the public imagination. There were TV shows, newspapers, and a spate of terrible Sci Fi movies about what might be travelling on, or in the wake of, the object.

There was a nationwide competition for schoolchildren, in years four, five, or six, to write either scientific essays about the object, and what comets were, or to write a creative description of what it might be like to visit the comet.

I entered the latter, writing a description of an ancient city, where the buildings, bridges, and walls, blended seamlessly with statues, the art and architecture inseparable. I described domed buildings, and towers like seashells, fortified canals and octagonal plazas.

Years later I would learn that Scamp had written something very similar.

So, I would discover, had quite a few other children.

*

That Christmas my class was sent on a school trip, to the Downs, to watch the comet as it passed through the sky, dazzling blue, and bright enough to blot out other stars. In Manchester, Scamp was watching from the top of a tower block, others gathered in Heaths, in parks, at events in the Peak District, Moors, New Forest, and in the Scottish Highlands.

It was haunting and beautiful.

It was also a shared experience for almost an entire generation. Every first date I ever went on, until I met Scamp featured the reliable ice breaker: Where did you see the Cartmel Object? Where did you go to watch it?

Shortly after the Object passed, the world rushed into Christmas, and life went on.

Aldred Road

The first recorded incidents of the Peeping Blurs came three years later. A local newspaper was the first to cover the odd hysteria at Aldred Road Secondary School, in Perivale, before the national press picked it up.

This is an excerpt from the original story.

Children Say The Scariest Things?

Local Parents are demanding action from teachers, after a spate of children claiming to be haunted by strange apparitions in the reflections of their mirrors.

Teachers at Aldred Road School are at a loss to where the story came from. One, who wishes to remain anonymous, told us: "You see this, from time to time. A story takes root, and passes between the kids, and they get scared enough to believe they saw something, but we can usually find the source. There is usually some story that has reached the school. It seemed odd to have the same image, the same suggestion, popping up three or four times in the same day, from different people, without a connecting thread between them."

In the last week, a number of kids have insisted they have glimpsed an intruder in the school, in the reflection of a mirror. The intruder is described as being tall and thin, wearing clothes whose colours blur, with a featureless egg in place of a face.

A complete search of the school, grounds, and surrounding streets was carried out before children began to suggest that the thing that had been watching them was inside the mirrors.

In the days since, several students from years Seven, Eight, and Nine, have complained of being awoken at night by blank faced figures menacing them from within the mirrors in their bedrooms.

Parents have blamed the strange hysteria for incidents of sleep walking, insomnia and panic attacks.

*

Sophie McCoy was a year Seven student at the time of the scare. She is now a solicitor, specialising in criminal law, from a practise in Tonbridge Wells. She meets me in her office, and waves me to the comfy seats by a coffee table, offering me a very confident smile.

"So," she says, rubbing the back of her neck, "where do you want me to begin?"

I look at her. "You were off sick that week?"

Sophie nods. "Yeah. I missed on the first few days of confusion, and hadn't heard any of the stories. There was a bug going around my Dad's work. He got off lightly with it, but it hit me bad for a week. I was pretty much a prisoner in my own bed. Anyway, in the evening my mum left the door to my room open, so we could talk, while she was busy about the flat. My sister was in her room, watching the telly, but her door swung open, and… Tina, my sister, had a mirror in her room, this huge old dress mirror she dragged from a skip. She was dead proud of it. I have to admit, after she had worked some magic on the frame, with silver paint and inks, it did look pretty sweet. Anyway, I am laying there, listening to music, playing with my camera, trying not to feel sorry for myself, when I see movement in the corner of my eye. I look over, and… I can't see Tina in her room, but I can see her in her reflection in the mirror, laying on her bed, staring at the TV, and this… thing is leaning over her. I scream at her, to look out, to get away, but she just looks confused, and can't understand my screams and tears."

"The thing?" I ask.

Sophie hands me a little square photograph from an instant camera. "I didn't even realise I had triggered the camera, until my mum and sister were worrying over me, thinking the fever had sent me delirious. Then… then Mum saw the picture, and was screaming too."

The photograph shows a doorway, through which a another door, from which a girl, Tina, is stepping out. She has a worried expression, and is dressed down and casual. Over her shoulder is a dress mirror, and in the mirror is… something.

The something is human shaped. It appears to be a tall, thin, almost skeletal man, in a high collared tunic, shiny and dark. The thing appears to have a head, a blank masque with no nose, or eyes, or distinguishable feature, a smooth egg, not quite flesh coloured.

It is an image that I can not easily explain. "Perhaps… some clothes hanging in the room, slightly out of focus? Or the television, or…"

Sophie gives me a sad look. "I wish."

I hand the photograph back. "And when did you hear about the other kids?"

"That night," Sophie says. "Of course, as soon as Mum saw the photograph, we were out of the flat, and staying at the safety of her friend's place, two doors down. We called the police, and they told us about the calls they had been having since the night before, and the kids all thinking they had seen this… ghost, but Mum waved the photographs under their nose and told them it wasn't a ghost in her flat, it was somebody in a Halloween mask threatening us! They didn't find him, but… I will never forget the look in the eyes of the police officers as they wondered if this wasn't a ghost story after all, if they had been dismissing something real as a…hoax?"

"How do you feel, looking at the picture?"

"Afraid," Sophie confesses. "I don't know what it was. I don't know how it got in our flat. How… if… it could have hurt us. How to defend myself if it comes back." She rubs her face. "Since then, I spoke to other kids, and… They all believe they saw something. Their fear was, is, real."

I hesitate. "Can I ask something else?"

"Yes."

"Do you remember the Cartmel Object?"

Sophie smiles. "Yeah. I remember that. I saw it on the Heath."

"Did you do the story writing competition?"

Sophie nods. "Yeah. I wrote… what it would be like to visit the comet."

"What did you say?"

She laughs. "Well, actually, I imagined a city with… statues, and domes, and…"

I tap open my phone and show her the picture that Scamp painted when she was at art college, the view of the city rendered with an airbrush.

Sophie nods. "Yes! That was… how? How did you know?"

I give her a sad smile. "It was a theory we found in one of the groups. I was just… seeing if it held up."

"What kind of a theory?" Sophie asks.

I flush. "The kind that I probably shouldn't tell you, if I want to keep any credibility."

*

Over three weeks sixteen children claim to have had close encounters with the figures in the mirror. When the story is picked up by the national press it quickly becomes apparent that there have been a handful of other sightings throughout London.

Perhaps because of the press attention, dozens of sightings are reported across Greater London. A consistent flow of sightings will continue until the end of term, and into the holidays.

As schools across the country broke up for Easter, the stories began to take an increasingly bizarre turn.

The Mischief Phase

Grace and Dee join us for dinner, bringing with them an old shoebox, that they promise will rock my world.

I go into the spare room to dig out my box files full of clippings and printouts.

Cracker and Jack are playing with the dress mirror again, pawing at their reflections, and pressing their noses to the glass, leaving a band of smudges across the bottom. Apparently it is hours of fun for the little guys.

I take my cuttings downstairs, and start setting out the clippings in (as best as I can tell) the order in which the events happened rather than the order they were reported in the press. The clippings are culled from many local papers from across London, and a few nationals.

"With a couple of weeks off school," I explain, "the kids who had been talking about figures in their mirrors, began to report other phenomena. In Lewisham there was a rash of poltergeists, with five different families reporting furniture being moved in their house, and small objects, usually toys or plates and glasses, being thrown around the houses and flats. In Bromley four different children fell sick with an unidentified fever."

These short bursts of unusual, unexplained, activity, so closely related to the schools where sightings of the Mirror People had been so common, were sometimes called the "Mischief Phase", although that puckish word suggests something considerably less harrowing than the experiences reported.

Scamp cocks her head. "What about the kids at Aldred Road?"

Dee grins. "That was what we were working on."

I show my wife some of the stories. "Well… their toys kept going…weird."

Scamp frowns at me. "What sort of weird?"

Dee answers before I can. "Burned. Broken. Twisted. Kids would be playing with their toys, would look up when their parents spoke to them, maybe only for a second, but when they looked back, it was all… kind of wrong."

Grace holds up the box. "You know, we could just show you… We borrowed these, but we have to give them back."

Inside the box are ten small toy cars, or rather three toy cars, and three pieces of rusting, burned, and exploded remnants that used to be toy cars. The paint has been scorched off the die cast toys, the plastic parts are gone. The metal shell has popped open.

Grace sighs. "They guy who loaned us these said he left his toys in the sitting room to go get a drink, and when he walked back in, they looked like they had survived a nuclear bomb."

Scamp turns one round in her fingers. "What could do this?"

"Fire," Dee answers. "A blacksmith's furnace."

Some of my clippings have photographs, of bikes, dolls, and even furniture and spots in the carpet had apparently burned without burning, in a matter of seconds.

Scamp considers the evidence. "So… is this one effect happening to lots of groups, but manifesting in different ways, or… lots of effects happening at the same time?"

"We don't know," I admit. "But, if they are different effects, we know they are grouped based on social connections, rather than geography. Here we have two kids, on the same street. One living there full time, one staying with her dad for the weekend. One gets the fever, one gets the poltergeist activity, associated with their respective schools, but their houses are a few meters apart."

Scamp sifts through the clippings. "There are…
dozens of these. I knew it was a big deal, I remember all
the TV specials, but… I had no sense of the scale."

"And," Grace adds, "remember all this time, kids
were still seeing the Mirror People, all through the
holidays."

Scamp looks at me. "And these kids? Did they all
write about the same city?"

I nod.

Scamp shudders. "The city I wrote about?"

"Yes," I tell her, "but we weren't in London, so…"

"But," she whispers, "we are now."

The telephone rings. We let the answer machine
get it.

It's the scratchy sea shanty and the screaming
again.

I cut it off.

Scamp rubs her face. "Well, that doesn't make me feel any better. So, this all happened right up until the kids started disappearing, right?"

We nod.

"So…" Scamp slumps in a seat. Cracker slinks into the room, and hops up onto her lap.

"So," Grace says, "we have to talk about that next, right?"

The Vanishing

In the evening of November Ninth, an unprecedented press conference was held in London, timed to be broadcast live within the Six O Clock news bulletin on every major channel in the UK. It was confirmed, that within an hour of each other, reports had been raised of thirteen children having gone missing from secondary schools across the capital.

Large photographs of the children, with descriptions of their school uniforms were displayed, and appeals were made for the children, or any who knew of their location, to come forwards.

The incidents were being treated as linked.

A member of the press asked if the connection was because the thirteen had previously been known to press in relation to their supernatural claims.

The Police stated calmly that every possible lead or connection would be investigated, but it was too early to speculate.

It was three nail biting days before the children were found, together, in Greenwich park, after one used a phone box to ring home and ask to be collected. The children were sunburned, dehydrated, and disorientated, unable to explain how they ended up in the park, or where they had been.

For a few weeks, the papers were filled with groundless speculation, that was all gleeful bluster without substance. Interest had faded away, and the mystery all but forgotten, long before the case was quietly closed with no firm conclusions.

An official enquiry into the investigation trundled on for years, and failed to make any stir when it too was released without firm conclusions.

It was five years later, before Jenny Halle, one of the Vanished, then twenty years old, volunteered to undergo the Hodgkinson Rae method, to try and retrieve her memories.

Excerpts from her sessions were broadcast on a TV special, reigniting interest in the mystery for a brief time.

They make uncomfortable watching.

The following a brief extract from the transcript of the sessions.

The bell rings for break.

I go to my locker and drop off my bag. I intend to go out and hang with my friends, but my hair is a mess. I step into the girls washroom, to splash my face, and straighten my hair.

There is somebody in the mirror.

I had begun to believe that the Mirror People had just been... well... they couldn't be real could they? But there it is, looking over my shoulder. I turn, and there is nobody in the room with me, but it is still in the mirror, and it grabs me, and drags me... It pulls me into the mirror.

[YOU TRAVEL THROUGH THE MIRROR?]

I... fall into the mirror. I fall upwards, like I'm... weightless. I have butterflies in my stomach, and I plunge through the glass like it is liquid. I can't breathe. I panic. The... THING covers my mouth, and... I am not in the bathroom. It was the bathroom in the reflection, but that isn't where I am now.

[WHERE ARE YOU?]

On a sort of pier, a stone and iron pier, but it isn't stood over the ocean. It stands over rubble, and ruins, and.. deep muddy craters. The air is thick and it chokes me. It stinks, and tastes horrible, like... rotting meat and vinegar. The THING drags me to the edge of the pier. They want me to see. I don't want to see, but they want me to see...

[WHAT DO THEY WANT YOU TO SEE?]

It sits in the sky and fills the horizon, feeding on the dead. It looks like a jellyfish, but made out of liquid silver, and its tentacles hang over the city, rooted in the mountain of dead bodies, being fed by trains and bulldozers.

This is what it does. It waits just outside the world, brining the world slowly to the boil, over decades. It seeds anguish, and violence, pollution and greed. It lets us turn the world to a powder keg, and when the atmosphere is good and rich, it lights the match.

Then it feeds.

The dead world is nearly exhausted. It will come to us next. We are almost ready. We are greedy, we are angry, we are divided and we hate. We pollute, and consume, and soon we will be desperate.

Then it will come...

None of the other Vanished have commented on the statements. They seem to make a point of avoiding the public eye, and I can only hope they have left their experiences behind, and live normal lives.

Speculation and lore seemed happy to continue without their input.

Several 'experts' have made predictions of when the world will end, based on their interpretation of Halle's vision. Most of those predictions have been and passed.

*

Doctor James Richards shows us to a couch in his private practise, on the top floor of a grand, brownstone town house. The office is brightly lit, and comfortable, in pastel shades, with deep leather seats, and frosted glass furniture.

Richards is long and thin, with an interesting face, and flint dark eyes. He sips his tea, and tilts his head. "I understand you are looking into the Hodgkinson Rae process?"

Scamp gestures for me to answer.

I nod. "I understand one of its uses is to help reconstruct memories?"

Richards smiles. "To a certain extent. You have to understand it is an analytical tool, and is more about understanding the patient's...subjective experience of a memory. It is probably best is we begin with the basics. If I told you to close your eyes, and focus on a memory, a very vivid memory... What would you choose?"

I glance at Scamp.

She hides her smile behind her fingers, because we both know the answer to that.

"Our first date," I say.

Richards looks at me. "Did it go well?"

"No!" I laugh. "I was nervous, and made bad jokes, and was… a complete idiot."

Scamp nods. "He was."

Richards laughs. "You can picture it now?"

"Yes." I squeeze Scamp's hand. "I can see the pub, and the autumn day, and I can see the moment we recognised each other, and…"

"Because," Richards says, his voice softening, "those were the moments when you were excited, or nervous, and your heart was running fast. The moments when your heart fluttered, and you forgot how to speak? Or gabbled too much?"

Scamp laughs. "Yes."

Richards gestures. "The memory is built around those feelings. We think the memory is a snapshot taken of the moment, and from that we remember the emotions, but it is the other way around. We record the emotions, and we tag them with a description of the moment. Then… when we remember the moment, we feel the emotions, and our brains rebuilds the moment from the notes, from… our imagination. We dream our memories into being. There are two factors that define the memory: the strength of the emotions, and the details we have noted on the tag. But… this is where it gets complicated. There are lots of things that can subtly nudge at, and slightly change the tag, from the way we talk about it, to… the way we hear others talk about it, or even the way a question is asked. They slightly shift our perceptions."

I look at him. "Like the experiment where students were convinced they went on a particular ride on holiday, that didn't exist?"

Richards puffs out his cheeks. "At an extreme level, but more often it is… much more subtle." He moves on. "Anyway, the Hodgkinson Rae process, when used correctly, can help identify the aspects of a memory that are… certain. The core details, that you then build upon and flesh out when you actively remember. In simple terms, we monitor your brain, and look for the bits that flash in a different area."

Scamp raises her hand. "You say when used correctly?"

"It is possible to pull on the wrong thread," Richards explains, "and… muddy the results. Especially if you think the process is there to detect truth, or lie, instead of understanding perception."

I check my notes. "What about recovering memories?"

"That is… possible," Richards says. "The process has been used to identify triggers that might draw out memories. Although that is far more…experimental." He pauses. "Although… if you wanted some good content for the podcast we could always experiment. Is there something you can't remember?"

Scamp snorts a laugh. "Yeah. What happened that day in Neale Lane? Where did you go?"

I sigh. "I told you, I just stepped into the other room. It can't have been more than a few seconds."

Scamp gives Richards a look.

"Okay," Richards says. "I could put you in the chair. We will put you into a trance like state, and we can see if we can solve this little mystery."

Scamp nudges me.

"Sure," I agree. "Why not?"

Memory Lane

The chair is much like a dentist chair, but for the plastic halo, with the blue lights, that sits around my crown. The room is bare, with plain walls. A projector hangs from the ceiling.

Scamp is with Richards in the control room next door.

"We shall begin," Richards announces. "Please try to relax."

The chair hums as it rises, and tilts back.

The lights dim, and the projector glows. Images of waves crashing against a sea wall cover the walls. A soft sound ebbs and flows in time with the waves, and without intending to, my breathing falls in time with the sounds, slow and steady, easing me down into a relaxed state.

The lights flicker and pulse.

I close my eyes, but am still aware of the lights flickering, as I sink down into the chair, and keep sinking.

An hour later, I am woken from my trance, and Scamp clings hold of me.

"What?" I ask, brushing away her tears. "What happened?"

"You…" She clears her throat. "You have to listen to the tape."

*

[ARE YOU COMFORTABLE?]

Yes.

[DO YOU REMEMBER NEALE LANE STATION?]

Yes.

[PICTURE IT FOR ME. YOUR WIFE GOES TO
LOOK IN THE WAITING ROOM. YOU OPEN THE
GENTS CLOAKROOM. WHAT DO YOU SEE?]

An old dusty toilet. There are stalls. Sinks covered
in grime and some rust stains. A mirror. Shadows. I
step inside, look around, and...

[TELL ME ABOUT THE MIRROR]

It runs the length of the room above the sinks. I
see myself, ugly as ever and...

[YOUR HEART IS RACING. WHAT DID YOU
SEE?]

A man.

[OTHER THAN YOURSELF?]

Yes.

[WHO?]

A man who is not old, but is bald, and dark eyed. He is dressed in dark clothes, old clothes. He stares at me, and I do not want to see him. I don't want to go with him.

[GO WITH HIM?]

I do not want to see.

[YOU HAVE SEEN HIM BEFORE?]

No. Yes. Many times… but I am not to remember. I can't remember.

[WHERE DO YOU SEE HIM?]

In the mirror at home. While Scamp sleeps. While I sleep. He… calls to me.

[YOU SLEEP WALK?]

Yes.

[HE CALLS TO YOU. DOES HE SPEAK?]

No. There is music. And old song, a sailor's song.

[AND YOU GO WITH HIM?]

I fall upwards into the light.

[AND WHAT IS IN THE LIGHT?]

They are not people. They are too tall... and bend in the wrong places. They have... smooth silver clothes and blank eggs where there should be a face. They hold me down. They pin me down. Machines like tentacles unfold from the light. They have needles on the end.

[DO THEY HURT YOU?]

Please, let me go. Please no. No! No! Please God no! No! Help! Help! Get off! No!

[DO THE NEEDLES HURT YOU?]

He is putting something in my head! There is something in the needles! And he laughs. He asks if I know his name.

[AND DO YOU?]

Restrim! He... leans over me. He warns me.

[WARNS YOU?]

Humanity has done its job. It is almost time for his master to come and claim us.

[I WANT YOU TO WAKE UP NOW}

It's in my head. I can feel the cold under my skin. What have they done to me? WHAT HAVE THEY DONE TO ME?

*

I stop the tape, not wanting to hear any more.

Scamp looks at me. "What was that?"

I shake my head. "The… process can be flawed. You said yourself, pull at the wrong thread, and…"

Richards holds up a hand. "You do not believe that?"

I shake my head,

He steps closer. "May I?"

Before I can answer, he brushes my hair apart, and looks at something.

Scamp sobs. She touches something on my scalp. Something painful.

Sores, that I did not know were there.

Richards points to a screen. "I want you to wait here, while I talk to a hospital. It could be nothing, but the scans identified some… anomalies."

"Anomalies?" I ask.

Richards looks at me. "I want to get you x-rayed. I think… there may be a problem."

Part Five: Where We Are Now

There are nine problems.

Three of them were new problems, under fresh sores in my scalp. The rest were older, hidden beneath scars that had long ago faded. The problems were studs of metal, the size of grains of rice, embedded in the outer surface of my cranium and occipital bones.

The objects were removed in surgery.

The Shut Down

The Government found me soon after my surgery.

Scamp and I spent the few weeks I was booked off to recover in Wales, staying with my parents, which was where the people from the Government found us.

There were two of them, smartly dressed, square shouldered, and starched. Their Home Office ID said they were both named Pipes, but I doubt that was their real name. They were armed with a search warrant, and escorted by some policemen, who waited outside, as Mum put the kettle on.

One of the Pipes saw my memento from the hospital, one of the metal studs, in a plastic tube. He held it up to the light. "I am afraid we have to take this."

"We also need to see any material you have for the podcast," the other explained. "Or is that with your friends? I believe Miss Pipes will be seeing them as we speak."

Scamp gave me a look, and we reluctantly held over my laptop.

The Pipes copied everything, and studied the material, asking many questions. There were a few passages that they deleted.

I was handed a bottle of pills.

The elder of the Pipes looked me in the eye. "You should be safe to return home. We have arranged for these pills to be delivered to you monthly. You will need to take two, with a meal, once a day. There is a telephone number on the bottle. If you notice the needle skipping… any lost time, even if you think you just dozed off, please call, and tell us. If you suffer nightmares, or see anybody in a mirror who is not there, please call us."

Scamp's gaze is cold and hard. "You… know about this?"

The Pipes do not answer.

Scamp covers her mouth. "This has happened before? It… still happens?"

The younger Pipes grimaced. "We are not at liberty to say."

Scamp gestured at the computer. "Are we allowed to use this, or…?"

"This?" The Elder Pipes sighed. "Yes. If you were…still inclined?"

Scamp gave me a look that suggested that she had no more enthusiasm for investigating than I did.

And just like that, the project was over.

But…the story was not.

Not quite.

*

"Have you seen the news?" Dee asks, over the phone.

I have just made it home from work, and haven't even taken my shoes off. Cracker and Jack are watching from the top of the stairs.

Our new home is a modern house on a new estate. Our lives are still packed in boxes. The floors are bare concrete, as we haven't had the flooring laid yet.

"What news?" I ask.

"Go look!" Dee insists.

"Okay." I flick on the TV. "Which channel?"

"Any!" Dee insists.

The picture swims to life.

My heart stops.

The Cartmel Object has changed course, and is moving towards Earth. It will take a few years to reach us, but an awful lot of people are wondering how that can even be possible.

I hurry back out the house to meet Scamp from work.

We spend the evening holding each other, watching the stars.

One glows brighter in the sky than the others.

Other Fallowgrave Tales You May Enjoy:

<u>The Fallowgrave Sequence</u>:

Fallowgrave (The Past Is Not Dead)

Fallowgrave: A Nightmare Heart

Fallowgrave: The Sleep Of The Just

Fallowgrave: The Blood Of Lambs

<u>Fallowgrave Tales</u>:

The Judas Tree

A Promise Once Made

Of Christmases Past

Macabre

Speechless

In Darkness Lies

www.ingramcontent.com/pod-product-compliance
Lightning Source LLC
Chambersburg PA
CBHW061530120726
48001CB00004B/1467